E.T.
The Extra-Terrestrial

William Kotzwinkle

Based on a screenplay by Melissa Mathison

Level 2

Retold by Michael Nation
Series Editors: Andy Hopkins and Jocelyn Potter

Pearson Education Limited
Edinburgh Gate, Harlow,
Essex CM20 2JE, England
and Associated Companies throughout the world.

ISBN: 978-1-4082-0950-9

First published in the U.S. by Berkeley Books, New York 1982
First Penguin Readers edition published 2002
This edition published 2009

1 3 5 7 9 10 8 6 4 2

Illustrations by Fabián Mezquita

The moral rights of the authors have been asserted in accordance with
the Copyright Designs and Patents Act 1988

Set in 12/15.5pt A. Garamond
Printed in China
SWTC/01
Produced for the Publishers by AC Estudio Editorial S.L.

Published by Pearson Education Ltd in association with Penguin Books Ltd,
both companies being subsidiaries of Pearson Plc

Acknowledgements
We are grateful to the following for permission to reproduce photographs:
The publisher would like to thank the following for their kind permission to reproduce their photographs:
(Key: b-bottom; c-centre; l-left; r-right; t-top)
Alamy Images: F1 on-Line 59bl; Leslie Garland Picture Library 31 (4); **DK Images:** 59c;
Getty Images: 59tr; NBC Inc 58; **Ronald Grant Archive:** 1, (pgiv), 31 (1 & 2), 48b, 48c, 51, 53, 54,
56; Amblin Entertainment 2, 7, 14, 16, 18-19, 32, 38l, 43, 46, 48t, 50; Universal City Studios 37, 38r;
iStockphoto: Plesea Petre 59br; **PunchStock:** FStop 31 (3); Goodshot 59tl

Every effort has been made to trace the copyright holders and we apologise in advance
for any unintentional omissions. We would be pleased to insert the appropriate
acknowledgement in any subsequent edition of this publication.

For a complete list of the titles available in the Penguin Active Reading series please write to your local
Pearson Longman office or to: Penguin Readers Marketing Department, Pearson Education,
Edinburgh Gate, Harlow, Essex CM20 2JE, England.

Contents

	Activities 1	iv
Chapter 1	The Extra-Terrestrial	1
Chapter 2	In the Yard	6
	Activities 2	10
Chapter 3	Elliott Finds E.T.	12
Chapter 4	Elliott's House	15
	Activities 3	20
Chapter 5	Elliott's Family	22
Chapter 6	Gertie's Computer	26
	Activities 4	30
Chapter 7	E.T. Makes a Transmitter	32
Chapter 8	In the Forest	35
	Activities 5	38
Chapter 9	E.T. Waits	40
Chapter 10	The Scientists	43
	Activities 6	48
Chapter 11	E.T. and the Spaceship	50
	Talk about it	56
	Write about it	57
	Project: Friends and Neighbors	58

1.1 What's the book about?

1 **Look at the picture on the front of this book and talk to another student.**

a What can you see? What is strange about one of the hands in the picture?
b Do you know anything about the movie of *E.T.*? What kind of story is it? Do people laugh or cry when they see the movie? Why?

2 **Look at this picture of E.T. How is he different from a person? Which of these are very different? Which are almost the same?**

| eyes |
| mouth |
| nose |
| head |

a very different: ....

b almost the same: ....

1.2 What happens first?

Look at page 1. Read the name of the chapter and the sentences in *italics*. Look at the picture. Then circle the best words in these sentences.

1 E.T. feels *happy / sad*.

2 He is *near / a long way away from* home.

3 He wants to be with his *friends / family*.

4 He *can / can't* get home.

CHAPTER 1

The Extra-Terrestrial

He looked sadly at it. His friends were in that spaceship, and
he was a long, long way from home.

The **space**ship came slowly down to **Earth**. It was round and beautiful, and its lights shone warmly in the night. The door opened and the **extra-terrestrial**s walked out. They were small and fat, so they couldn't walk fast.

space /speɪs/ (n) Around our world, and a long way away, other worlds move in *space*. Some people think that *spaceships* come here from other worlds.
Earth /ɜːθ/ (n) *Earth* is our home—our world.
extra-terrestrial /ˌekstrətəˈrestriəl/ (n) An *extra-terrestrial* is a life—maybe a person—from another world.

They looked around them at the **plant**s. The extra-terrestrials often came to Earth. They loved plants. They talked quietly to them, and then they took them home.

The night was dark. The spaceship stood in a **forest** and the visitors worked quietly. But some men heard the spaceship come to Earth. They were **scientist**s and they wanted to find it. They got in their **van**s and drove to the forest.

One extra-terrestrial spoke some kind words to a small tree, and then pulled it from the ground. He loved Earth. He was **million**s of years old and he knew the plants well. He wanted to know the people, too. But that was difficult. Earth people didn't really understand extra-terrestrials.

The old visitor walked away from the spaceship. When he walked past a friend, warm red lights shone from their **heart**s.

The extra-terrestrial walked to the end of the forest. The yellow lights of a small town shone through the trees. Who was inside the houses?

---

plant /plænt/ (n) *Plants* give us food, and we cut flowers from plants for our houses.
forest /ˈfɒrɪst, fɑr-/ (n) A *forest* is a place with a lot of trees.
scientist /ˈsaɪəntɪst/ (n) We know more all the time because *scientists* do tests.
van /væn/ (n) People drive a *van* because they want to carry a lot of things in the back.
million /ˈmɪlyən/ (number) A *million* is 1,000,000.
heart /hɑrt/ (n) When your *heart* stops, you are going to die. People say that your feelings come from your heart.

What did Earth people do in them? This was the extra-terrestrial's last night on Earth and he wanted to know. On the trip back through space, he could tell his friends about Earth people.

He found a road and walked across it. It felt strangely hard under his feet and he couldn't walk fast. Then, he heard his friends in the spaceship.

"We're leaving. Come back," they called.

The extra-terrestrial listened. No, he had more time. He was near the town now and his heart-light shone again. He felt excited. He could talk to the Earth people. He could teach them.

Then, his friends called again from the spaceship.

"They know we're here. It's dangerous! It's dangerous! Come back! We're leaving now!"

The old visitor felt it, too—he had to go. He couldn't run fast. He turned back, but there were a lot of cars on the road. They went very fast and their lights shone in his eyes. He couldn't see. He ran into the forest, through the trees.

"This way, this way ..." the plants told him.

There was the spaceship. A friend stood in the open door. The extra-terrestrial ran as fast as he could. He could see his friend's heart-light.

"Where are you?" it called.

"I'm coming, I'm coming ..." he answered, and he ran out of the trees.

Then, the little extra-terrestrial felt something in his heart. He was afraid. He ran quickly. He saw the beautiful lights of the spaceship—above him, in the dark night sky. It flew up and up. He looked sadly at it. His friends were in that spaceship, and he was a long, long way from home.

◆

Mary sat in her bedroom. She read her newspaper, and she listened to her two sons, Elliott and Michael. They were in the kitchen with some friends. The boys sat at the table and played a game. They made a lot of noise.

"I run down the road," Elliott said excitedly. "They come after me, and they're really near ..."

Mary felt unhappy. "No husband," she thought, "and I can't understand my children. What *are* they talking about? But they're excited and happy. When am *I* excited? When am I in love?"

CHAPTER 2

In the Yard

A door opened and one of the Earth people took the food.
"Look, that's Elliott," the plant said. "He lives here."

T he extra-terrestrial walked slowly back down the road to the town. There was a wall in front of him, so he climbed over it. He fell heavily on the ground and then looked up. He was in the yard of one of the houses.

"What am I doing?" he thought.

There were some plants in the yard. He went to one and put his arms around it.

"What can I do?" he asked.

"Go to the window," the plant said. "Look inside."

"That's a bad idea," E.T. thought. He was on Earth now because he wanted to look in windows.

"Go," said the plant.

The extra-terrestrial walked to the window and looked into the kitchen. Five Earth people sat around a table in the middle of the room. They had some small cards in their hands. They shouted, and then they moved things across the table.

This was a very strange place. He understood nothing! Tired and sad, the extra-terrestrial went back to the plants and sat down.

"Tomorrow they will find me," he thought, "and that will be the end."

Suddenly a van drove into the yard, and the extra-terrestrial felt afraid again.

"It's OK," a plant told him. "It's only bringing food for the people inside."

The van stopped in front of the house. A door opened and one of the Earth people took the food.

"Look, that's Elliott," the plant said. "He lives here."

◆

Elliott looked into the yard and saw—something ... Quickly, the little visitor put his hand over his heart-light and **hid** in the dark. He waited. What now? Then an orange flew at him and hit him near the heart. Him—millions of years old, and a great extra-terrestrial ... Angrily, he threw the orange back into the night. The Earth person cried out and ran into the house.

"Help! Mom! Help!" Elliott shouted.

Mary felt afraid.

hide /haɪd/ (v) You *hide* when you don't want people to find you.

"There's something out there! It threw an orange at me!" Elliott said.

"Ooooo!" said Tyler, a friend of Elliott. "An orange! Very dangerous!"

Elliott's mom, Mary, took a light, and then she and the boys went into the yard.

"What did you see?" Mary asked Elliott.

"Something there," he answered. He **point**ed to the end of the yard.

Elliott's brother, Michael, said, "Look, something walked across the ground here!"

◆

The extra-terrestrial looked at them from the dark. There were five Earth children, and a tall, beautiful person. Strange sounds came from her mouth. He couldn't understand them. Was she their mother?

His heart-light started to shine, so he put his hand over it. She was the most beautiful of Earth people. The extra-terrestrial looked and looked.

"Stupid heart-light," he said—but it shone more and more.

The Earth people went back into the kitchen. Later in the night, three of the children left the house. They were Elliott's friends, Greg, Tyler, and Steve. Then, the lights went out and the house was quiet.

The extra-terrestrial walked across the yard to the plants. It was very dark now, so he couldn't see. He hit his head and fell back on the ground. He cried out loudly.

Suddenly, the kitchen door opened and Elliott ran out into the yard with his dog, Harvey. He shone a light into the plants and saw the extra-terrestrial. Elliott shouted—and fell over.

The extra-terrestrial started to run.

"Don't go!" Elliott said.

The boy spoke very quietly and the old visitor stopped. He turned and looked at the boy. Their eyes met.

"Don't go!" Elliott said again.

But the extra-terrestrial ran into the night.

---

point /pɔɪnt/ (v) You *point* at something with your finger when you want somebody to look at it.

2.1 Were you right?

Look back at your answers to Activity 1.2 on page iv. Then check (✓) the right sentences.

- 1 The spaceship leaves the extra-terrestrial on Earth.

- 2 He doesn't want to go on the spaceship.

- 3 He feels afraid without his friends.

- 4 The plants talk to him.

- 5 His heart-light shines for Elliott.

- 6 He is afraid of Elliott.

2.2 What more did you learn?

Find the names of Elliott's brother, his mother, his three friends, and his dog. Write them below. (There will be one box with nothing in it.)

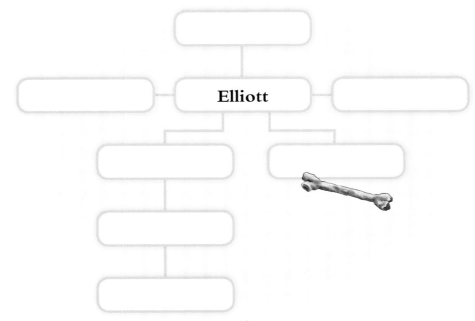

.3 Language in use

Look at the sentences on the right. Then
finish these sentences in the same way.
Use the words in the box.

> He looked **sadly** at it.
>
> Its lights shone **warmly** in the night.

quietly	slowly	quickly
loudly	angrily	heavily

1 The extra-terrestrials talk .... to the plants.

2 The little extra-terrestrial runs .... to the spaceship.

3 Then he walks .... to the town.

4 He falls .... from the wall into Elliott's yard.

5 He throws the orange .... at Elliott.

6 Elliott shouts ....

.4 What happens next?

The extra-terrestrial sees a lot of new things on Earth, but he doesn't
understand them. Which of these things will he be interested in? Talk
about it, and then write *Yes* or *No* under each picture.

1

....

2

....

3

....

4

....

5

....

6

....

CHAPTER 3

Elliott Finds E.T.

Suddenly, the boy's eyes opened. He looked up into the big eyes above him—very old eyes from a different world.

In the forest, the extra-terrestrial listened to the scientists. They looked carefully at everything.

"The spaceship was here, right here, and it got away. I lost it."

The most important scientist turned angrily and walked to his van. He wore a lot of **key**s. They made a loud noise when he walked.

The scientists climbed into their vans and drove out of the forest.

The extra-terrestrial looked sadly at the ground. Where was his spaceship now? He felt weak and hungry, and he didn't have any food.

"The end is near," he thought.

Then, he heard a sound.

Elliott, the Earth boy, came into the forest. The extra-terrestrial hid in the trees so the boy couldn't see him.

Elliott had a bag in his hand and he took a small round thing out of it. He put it on the ground and walked back a little way. He put a second thing on the ground and walked back again. Then, Elliott put down a third thing, and a fourth ... He walked back and back and put more things on the ground.

Now, the extra-terrestrial couldn't see him. He walked slowly out of the trees and looked at the first small thing on the ground. What was it? He turned it over in his hand.

The old visitor put it in his mouth. It was really good! He walked through the forest and happily ate the chocolates. He felt strong again.

After some time, the chocolates brought the extra-terrestrial back to Elliott's house. He found the boy asleep on the ground, next to the plants in the yard. The extra-terrestrial felt afraid and unhappy again.

key /kiː/ (n) After you turn a *key* in a door, people can't open it.

Suddenly, the boy's eyes opened. He looked up into the big eyes above him—very old eyes from a different world.

The extra-terrestrial looked down. The boy was very ugly. He had a big nose, big ears, and very small dark eyes. But he was afraid, too, and the extra-terrestrial felt sorry. He put out one long finger and **touch**ed the boy on the head.

Elliott shouted and jumped back. The extra-terrestrial jumped back, too. Then, he opened his hand and showed Elliott a chocolate. He pointed to it and then pointed to his mouth.

"OK," Elliott said.

He took out his bag of chocolates and put one on the ground, then another, across the yard. The extra-terrestrial ate them quickly. The chocolate ran out of his mouth, and it was on his fingers, too. He felt stronger and stronger.

The old visitor was in the house before he knew it, up the stairs and into the boy's bedroom. There the boy gave him a lot of chocolates.

"I'm Elliott," the boy said.

The extra-terrestrial didn't understand, but that wasn't important. The boy gave him chocolates—the boy was good. The old visitor felt very tired. He sat on the floor, and slowly went to sleep.

touch /tʌtʃ/ (v) When you *touch* something, you put your finger or your fingers on it.

CHAPTER 4

Elliott's House

"What am I going to call you?" Elliott looked into his big, old eyes.
"You're an extra-terrestrial, right? We'll call you E.T."

T he extra-terrestrial woke up the next morning.
"Where am I?" he thought.

"Come with me, you have to hide," Elliott said.

He pushed the extra-terrestrial across the room into a closet and then closed the door. Elliott jumped into bed before his mother came in the room. The extra-terrestrial watched Mary through the door.

"It's time for school, Elliott," she said.

"I'm sick, Mom ..."

"I have to go to work," she said. "Will you be all right? OK, you can stay home. But no TV—understand? You can't sit in front of it all day."

She went down for her breakfast. Elliott's brother, Michael, was in the

car outside. He liked driving, but he wasn't very good. His mother came out of the house and Michael got out of the car. Then Mary drove away.

Elliott got out of bed and opened the closet door. The extra-terrestrial moved back to the wall.

"Come out here," Elliott said.

He gave the old visitor his hand.

Slowly, the extra-terrestrial walked out of the closet and then looked around.

"What am I going to call you?" Elliott looked into his big, old eyes. "You're an extra-terrestrial, right? We'll call you E.T. Is that OK?"

E.T. looked at Elliott and answered him. Elliott felt the answer inside his head. It was a strange noise, but he couldn't understand it.

"Do you talk?" Elliott asked.

He made a mouth with his fingers and moved them up and down. E.T. moved his fingers, too.

"Do you like music?"

Elliott turned on the radio and a really loud noise came out. E.T. put his hands over his ears and put his head down.

Elliott showed E.T. some money.

"Here, see—this is a dollar," Elliott said.

E.T. looked at the paper in Elliott's hand. Was this more food? He put it in his mouth, then he took it out again.

"Right," Elliott said. "You can't eat that. Are you hungry again? I'm hungry. Let's have some food."

They went downstairs to the kitchen and Elliott made breakfast. E.T. watched Elliott carefully. The boy had a **fork** in his hand and he hit it on the table. *Click.* E.T. looked at the fork for a long time. Then he took it from the table. *Click, click, click.*

"What's happening?" Elliott asked. "Suddenly, I feel sad."

Elliott felt full of new things. They came from E.T., but Elliott didn't understand them.

E.T. closed his eyes. *Click, click, click.* Maybe his friends could hear the sound of the fork, high up in the sky. But how?

Elliott didn't want to feel sad.

"We're going to have a good day," he said, and he took E.T.'s hand. "Come with me ..."

The long fingers closed around Elliott's hand and Elliott felt strange again. Was E.T. a young child? Yes, but he was very old, too. Something inside Elliott changed. E.T. was a child of the **star**s, and now he was, too.

---

fork /fɔrk/ (n) In many countries people eat with a knife, *fork*, and spoon.
star /stɑr/ (n) The lights in the sky at night are *stars*.

They went back to Elliott's bedroom. Elliott opened the closet door and said, "We have to make a nice place for you in the closet. OK?"

E.T.'s eyes were on the window and the beautiful sunlight outside. Elliott made a bed for him in the closet. He had to help E.T. He didn't know why and he didn't ask. He had to help him or—or die.

"You'll like it in here," Elliott called through the door. He put some **toy**s at the front of the closet.

"Look," Elliott said. "People will think you're a toy, too. They won't see you."

E.T. looked inside, but he didn't understand. Elliott put a light on in the closet, but the light was too strong. E.T. had to close his eyes.

E.T. walked back, away from the light, and hit a **record-player**. The record on it turned around and around, and E.T. thought, "A fork ... the record-player turns ... I can talk to my friends ..."

He walked across Elliott's bedroom and looked in his desk. He started to throw things around the room.

"Oh, be careful. I have to have a clean bedroom," Elliott told him. He pulled E.T. slowly to the closet. "You stay in there, OK? Stay ..."

E.T. went into his little room and sat down quietly. Where were the spaceship and his friends? Elliott closed the closet door.

E.T. looked up at the light in the closet and thought of the spaceship. He had to talk to his friends. He remembered the fork ... its sound—*click, click, click* ... the record player ... around and around ...

toy /tɔɪ/ (n) Children play with *toys*.
record-player /'rɛkərd ˌpleɪər/ (n) Our grandparents used a *record-player* when they wanted to listen to music.

3.1 Were you right?

Look back at your answers to Activity 2.4. Then answer these questions.

1 What does Elliott give to E.T.? They make him feel happy.

....

2 What does E.T. try to eat? It isn't food.

....

3 Does E.T. like the radio and the light?

....

4 E.T. is very interested in these. What are they?

....

3.2 What more did you learn?

Put these in the right order. Write the numbers, 1–7.

◯   **a**   Elliott makes a bed for E.T. in the closet.

◯   **b**   E.T. touches Elliott on the head.

◯   **c**   Elliott's mother and brother drive away from the house.

_1_   **d**   The scientists leave the forest.

◯   **e**   E.T. sleeps in Elliott's bedroom.

◯   **f**   Elliott puts chocolates on the ground.

◯   **g**   E.T. thinks about a use for the record-player and the fork.

3 Language in use

Look at the sentences on the right. Then put the right prepositions in these sentences.

> The extra-terrestrial listened **to** the scientists.
>
> They looked carefully **at** everything.

1 The scientist walked .... his van.
2 The scientists climbed .... their vans.
3 Then the scientists drove .... the forest.
4 Elliott put a chocolate .... the ground.
5 E.T. found Elliott asleep, ... the plants.
6 E.T. had very old eyes—eyes .... a different world.
7 "Come .... me," Elliott said.
8 "It's time .... school," Mary said.
9 "You can't sit .... the TV all day."
10 E.T.'s long fingers closed .... Elliott's hand.

4 What happens next?

Answer these questions. What do you think?

1 Who is this little girl?

....

2 How old is she?

....

3 What does she do
on her computer?

....

....

4 Will she be afraid of E.T.?   ....

5 Will E.T. be afraid of her?   ....

6 Will Elliott's brother find E.T.?   ....

7 Will Elliott tell his mother?   ....

CHAPTER 5

Elliott's Family

"Is he from the stars?" she asked.
"Yes, he's from the stars."

"**M**ichael!"
"How are you?" Michael asked, and pushed past Elliott into his bedroom.

"I have to tell you something. It's really important," Elliott said.

"OK, be quick," Michael told him.

"Close your eyes."

"Why?" Michael asked.

"Do it, Michael!"

Elliott went into the closet and put his arm around E.T.

"Come and meet my brother," he said.

They walked out into the bedroom, and at the same time Elliott's little sister, Gertie, ran into the room, with Harvey the dog. She shouted

and E.T. made a loud noise. Michael opened his eyes—and he shouted, too.

"Elliott," he said, "we have to tell Mom."

"We can't, Michael. She'll do the right thing. And then what will happen?" Elliott pointed to E.T. "He'll be dog food."

Harvey looked interested.

"Does he talk?" Michael asked.

"No."

"What's he doing here?"

"I don't know," Elliott said.

The two boys looked at their five-year-old sister. She looked at E.T. with big eyes.

"Gertie, he won't hurt you," Elliott said. "You can touch him."

The children put their hands on E.T. He could see inside them through their fingers. They weren't stupid, but could they get him up to the stars?

"You can't tell anybody, Gertie—you can't tell Mom," Elliott said.

"Why not?" Gertie asked.

"Because—she can't see him," Elliott told her. "Only children can see him."

"That's not right," Gertie said. "I'm not a baby!"

Elliott took a toy from her hands. "Do you want me to break this, Gertie?"

"No. Is he from the stars?" she asked.

"Yes, he's from the stars."

◆

E.T. walked slowly around Elliott's bedroom. He wanted new things for his **transmitter**, but what? He looked again at the record-player. He put his finger on it and it moved around. How could he use the fork with this machine?

Elliott came into the room. He brought E.T. some fruit and vegetables.

"Here's some food," he said.

Gertie came in with some toys. She brought E.T. some flowers, too, and put them at his feet. E.T.'s heart-light shone happily.

"Thank you, little girl," he thought. "That is very nice of you."

Michael came in. Maybe E.T. wasn't there now—but, no, there he was.

"I have an idea," Elliott said.

He showed E.T. a picture of the world, and pointed to the United States.

"Look, we're here," he said. "Where are you from?"

E.T. understood. He looked out the window at the millions of stars in the sky. There were some balls on the floor. He put five balls around one big ball.

"Five? Are you from Jupiter?"

---

transmitter /trænz'mɪtə, 'trænz₁mɪtə/ (n) When somebody is a long way away, you can "talk" to them with a *transmitter*.

E.T. didn't understand the question. He pointed at the five balls. They went up above the children's heads. When E.T. put his hand down, the balls fell quickly to the floor again. Then, he went into the closet with his flowers.

♦

In the night E.T. looked up from his bed in the closet, and saw Elliott climb out the window.

"Where is he going?" E.T. thought.

He didn't want to think about that, so he put his head down again.

♦

Elliott hid in some plants by the road with Harvey and watched the scientists' vans. They drove up and down the streets, and then out into the forest. Their lights shone in the night sky.

"Harvey," Elliott said quietly, "we have something wonderful with us. Do you know that? I love him, Harvey."

He looked up at the sky. Which star did his new friend come from?

CHAPTER 6

Gertie's Computer

His little eyes shone and they looked carefully at Elliott.
Lance knew something, and Elliott was afraid.

Elliott and Michael walked to school.

"We have to tell, Elliott," Michael said.

"No," Elliott answered. "He wants to stay with us. Michael, listen, there are some strange people around here now. I don't know them. Look at that car. There's a man inside it and he's reading a newspaper. Why is he there? What's he waiting for? I think they're looking for E.T."

Elliott was very unhappy.

"Michael," he said, "we can't tell, or he won't get back home. I know it—I can feel it inside me."

Greg, Tyler, and Steve were at the bus stop.

"Elliott, what happened to your 'little man' in the yard? Did he come back?" Steve asked him.

"Yes, he came back," Elliott said too quickly, "and he wasn't a little man. He was a spaceman!"

"What? Who's a spaceman?" asked Lance, a small boy with red hair.

Lance pushed through the other boys. His little eyes shone and they looked carefully at Elliott. Lance knew something, and Elliott was afraid.

◆

Gertie had no school that day. She wanted to play with E.T., so she took a lot of her toys to his closet.

"Don't be afraid," she said. "I'm here. Now, here are my toys, and this is my computer. It teaches me better English."

E.T. took the computer in his long fingers. He thought quickly and his heart-light shone. Gertie started the computer and it spoke. E.T.

opened his eyes wide, and then they shone, too. Yes, now he could learn English, but more important—most important—this was a computer.

E.T. looked inside the machine. He could listen to the computer and learn English, but there was more. E.T. knew about computers. He could teach this computer to speak his language. Then, he could send the sound up to his friends in the stars.

◆

Later, Gertie put a funny hat on E.T.'s head.

"B," said E.T. "Be good."

The closet door opened and Elliott came in.

"Elliott," E.T. said, and Elliott's mouth fell open.

"I taught him to talk," said Gertie.

"You spoke to me!" said Elliott happily. "'E.T.' Can you say that? You're E.T."

They heard the telephone. It was Lance—and Lance never called Elliott.

"Hello, Elliott ..." Lance said. He wanted to know everything. Elliott could hear it in every word. "... yes, Elliott, space, space, space. I'm thinking about it now. Isn't that strange? Is something strange happening? I feel ..."

"I have to go ..."

Elliott put down the phone. Lance knew something, and that was dangerous.

E.T. pointed to the phone, and then to the window.

"What do you mean, E.T.?" Elliott asked.

Again, E.T. pointed to the phone and to the window.

"Phone home."

"You want to—phone home?" Elliott asked.

"E.T. phone home," the extra-terrestrial said.

4.1 Were you right?

Look back at your answers to Activity 3.1. Go back to Activity 2.2 and put Gertie's name in the last box. Then answer these questions.

1 What does Gertie give to E.T.? ....

2 How do you know that E.T. likes Gertie? ....

3 What does Michael want to do about E.T.? ....

4.2 What more did you learn?

Who is speaking? Match the names with their words.

Gertie	Lance	Elliott	E.T.	Michael

Are you from Jupiter?

1 ....

He'll be dog food.

2 ....

Does he talk?

3 ....

Here are my toys, and this is my computer.

4 ....

I taught him to talk.

5 ....

We can't tell, or he won't get back home.

6 ....

Phone home.

7 ....

What? Who's a spaceman?

8 ....

3 Language in use

Look at the sentence on the right. Then write the sentences below in the past.

> Elliott **went** into the closet and **put** his arm around E.T.

1 E.T. is making a loud noise.

....

2 They aren't stupid.

....

3 Can they get him up to the stars?

....

4 Elliott is taking a toy from her hands.

....

5 He is bringing E.T. some fruit and vegetables.

....

6 E.T. understands.

....

7 The ball is falling quickly to the floor again.

....

8 Elliott is hiding in some plants by the road.

....

4 What happens next?

The scientists are looking for E.T. Which of these will help them find him? How? Write ✓ or ✗ under each picture, and talk about them.

E.T. Makes a Transmitter

*E.T. felt happy and sad at the same time. He was only a toy
to her. How could she love him?*

E.T. worked on the inside of the computer. Now it didn't speak in English. It said, "*doopdoople, skiggle*," and "*zclock*," and other strange words. Earth people couldn't understand them.

The boys sat next to E.T. and he played them the new sounds on the computer.

"Is that your language, E.T.?" they asked him.

"E.T. phone home."

He pointed out the window of the closet.

"And they'll come?"

"Yes," E.T. told them.

But he had to have more things for his transmitter. When he put it below the stars, it had to play all day and all night. The boys brought him a lot of different things and E.T. worked very hard.

E.T.'s finger got very hot. He touched the record-player and the computer with his hot finger, and put some more things on them. Slowly, he built his transmitter.

"You have fire in your finger, E.T.!" Elliott said.

"More ... more ..." E.T. said.

"OK, we'll find you more things."

Elliott and Michael went away. E.T. worked hard and Gertie played with her toys. They didn't hear their mom on the stairs, and they didn't hear her outside the room. They only heard when she opened the door to Elliott's room.

E.T. had to hide. He jumped quickly into the line of toys at the front of his closet. Mary's eyes slowly moved over E.T. and the toys. She didn't see him. She turned away.

E.T. felt happy and sad at the same time. He was only a toy to her. How could she love him?

◆

Elliott was asleep in his bed when E.T. walked quietly out of the bedroom. He looked in Gertie's room. She loved him, but she loved her toys, too.

He walked to Mary's room. She was asleep and he watched her for a long time. She was the most beautiful woman in the world—the most beautiful woman in space. Quietly, he put a chocolate on the bed next to her head and then he left her room.

Harvey went with E.T. to the kitchen. E.T. had some milk and ate chocolate cake. Harvey wanted some food, too, so E.T. gave him some meat.

Harvey looked up at E.T.

"I'm your dog. I'll always help you," his eyes told the extra-terrestrial.

◆

There was a van near Elliott's house. It drove down the street and the scientists inside listened on their radios to the conversations in people's houses.

"Mom, we don't have any milk for ..."

And: "I'll be in tonight, Jack. Do you want to ..."

And: "His transmitter's ready, Michael. We can take it out and try it."

The van stopped and the scientist with the keys listened carefully.

"You know, Elliott, he's looking really sick."

"Don't say that, Michael. We're fine."

"What's this 'we'? You always say 'we' now."

"He can see inside me. I understand him. I feel I *am* him."

This conversation didn't mean anything to other people, but Keys and the other scientists understood everything now. Keys looked at a street map and he found Mary's house on it.

CHAPTER 8

In the Forest

E.T. moved his fingers, and the bike slowly left the ground.
It flew high over the small plants, then up higher over the trees.

E lliott told E.T. about Halloween.*
"You can walk around outside tonight and people won't look at you," he said. "Everybody will look strange. Oh, I'm sorry. Of course, you're not strange—but you're different."

Elliott put a hat on E.T.'s head, and shoes on his big feet. Then, he put some clothes on him.

"You look good," Elliott said.

Downstairs, Mary looked at E.T. and said, "Gertie, those are wonderful clothes. How did you get that fat stomach?"

She touched E.T.

"Oh, we put a lot of different things under her skirt," Elliott said.

He quickly pulled E.T. away into the garage. The transmitter was in the garage, in a box.

"OK, E.T., get on," Elliott said.

He and Michael put E.T. and his transmitter on Elliott's bike, then they **rode** out into the street. The street was full of Earth children in crazy clothes of all colors.

"Earth really is an interesting place," E.T. thought.

"Those are very strange clothes!" said a man at the door of his house.

In his hat and big shoes, with his fat stomach down to the floor and his big eyes, E.T. looked stranger than the children on the street. Everybody in the different houses spoke to him and talked about his clothes. E.T. really liked this after weeks in a closet. Also, people gave him a lot of candy.

---

* Halloween: the night of October 31. Children wear funny clothes. They go to houses around town and ask for candy.

ride /raɪd/ (v) You *ride* a bicycle when you want to go somewhere on it.

They rode from street to street and went to a lot of houses.

"OK," said Elliott. "Let's try that house over there."

The door opened and there stood Lance. E.T. felt afraid.

"Who's this?" Lance asked. "He's very strange."

He looked very carefully at E.T.

Elliott and E.T. walked away. They jumped up on the bike and E.T. said, "Fast."

"What will Lance do? Will he tell the scientists?" Elliott thought.

He looked back, but he couldn't see Lance. He turned his bike off the road and rode to the forest. E.T. thought quickly. He had to start his transmitter.

"Elliott—"

"Yes?"

"Here we go."

E.T. moved his fingers, and the bike slowly left the ground. It flew high over the small plants, then up higher over the trees.

After some time, they came down again in the middle of the forest. Elliott opened the box and took out the transmitter. Then, E.T. started it.

... geeple doople zwak-zwak snafn olg mnnnnin ...

Elliott listened carefully to the sound. It was very weak, and the sky was very big. Could anybody hear it?

E.T. looked at Elliott and understood. He touched the boy on his arm.

"We found a way," he said.

"We did?"

"Our sound is the way. It will find Them."

They stood quietly with their transmitter for a long time. The stars listened to the sounds—and, of course, near them in the trees, Lance listened, too.

5.1 Were you right?

Look back at your answers to Activity 4.4. What are these people doing in these chapters? Circle the right answers.

1 What are the scientists doing?

   listening   watching   driving

2 What is Lance doing?

   listening   looking   telling people

3 What is Elliott's mother doing?

   listening   watching   asking questions

5.2 What more did you learn?

The red words in these sentences are wrong. Write the right words.

1 E.T. worked on the back
  of the computer.

  ....

2 He made a television.

  ....

3 His foot got very hot.

  ....

4 Elliott and E.T. jumped on
  the transmitter.

  ....

5 It flew under the trees.

  ....

6 The sound from the transmitter
  was very strong.

  ....

5.3 Language in use

Look at the sentences on the right. Which sentences on the right follow the sentences on the left? Make longer sentences with *when*.

> **When** he put it below the stars, it had to play all day and all night.
>
> They only heard **when** she opened the door to Elliott's room.

1 E.T. asked for more things for his transmitter.

2 E.T. had to hide.

3 E.T. put a chocolate next to Mary.

4 Keys looked at a map.

5 People gave E.T. candy.

6 E.T. moved his fingers.

a Mary came into Elliott's bedroom.

b She was asleep.

c He went to their houses.

d He found Mary's house.

e The bike left the ground.

f The boys found them for him.

1 *When E.T. asked for more things for his transmitter, the boys found them for him.*

2

3

4

5

6

5.4 What happens next?

What do you think? Put these in the best order, from 1 for *very possible* to 6 for *not very possible*.

The transmitter stops.

Lance finds the transmitter.

The spaceship comes back.

The scientists find the transmitter.

Elliott gets sick.

E.T. dies.

CHAPTER 9

E.T. Waits

Michael pulled Elliott out of bed and took him to E.T.
The little extra-terrestrial was very, very sick.

Mary walked to the front door and opened it.
"... we heard about a spaceship ..." the man said.

Mary looked at his keys. The man showed her a card—he was an important scientist.

"I ... I'm sorry," she said, "but I don't understand ..."

"A spaceship came down near here. We think that an extra-terrestrial stayed on Earth," the scientist said.

"Is this a ... game?" she asked.

"No." His eyes looked coldly into hers. "It's not."

◆

E.T. felt weak and sad. After weeks, there was no answer from space. His friends were high up in the sky now, and they could hear nothing.

"We're dying," E.T.'s flowers told him.

He couldn't help them. They could feel E.T.'s sad heart, and he couldn't change that.

Elliott came home and saw E.T.'s gray face. He felt afraid. He sat down and took E.T.'s hand in his. What could he do? Every plant in the house was dead. Everything felt heavy and tired.

"You can get better," Elliott told him. "You can do anything."

E.T. looked at Elliott.

"Carry me ... a long way away ..." he said slowly, "... and leave me ..."

"E.T.," Elliott answered, "I'll never leave you."

E.T. spoke to Elliott again. He had to tell him.

"I am ... very dangerous to you ..." He pointed with his finger "... and to your world ..."

He looked up, and his star-eyes shone.

"But our transmitter is working every day," said Elliott.

"Trash."

E.T.'s eyes shone again in the dark.

"You're not trying," Elliott said, afraid of those eyes. "Please, E.T."

That night E.T. was grayer, and Elliott felt sad, too. He felt heavier and heavier and his head hurt. Everything was dark. In the gray light of morning Elliott looked at E.T. and his friend was almost white.

Elliott walked slowly to Mary's room. She looked at him and said, "What's wrong?"

"Everything—is nothing," Elliott said sadly.

"Oh, baby, don't say that," Mary said, but really she felt bad, too.

"I have something wonderful," Elliott said, "but now it's sad."

"Everybody feels that sometimes," Mary said.

The warm bed was better than words, and Elliott got in next to her.

There was something in the house, in its center—something strange, with no name. Mary felt it.

"Can you ... tell me about it?" she asked.

"Later ..." Elliott said.

"Go to sleep," Mary said, and put her hand on his head. "Go to sleep."

◆

The next morning Michael tried to wake Elliott, but it took a long time.

"What's happening?" Michael thought.

Elliott was sick, and everything in the house felt bad. Michael pulled Elliott out of bed and took him to E.T. The little extra-terrestrial was very, very sick.

"We have to tell now, Elliott," said Michael. "We have to get help."

"No, you can't, Michael. Don't ..."

The world couldn't know about them. The scientists wanted to take E.T. away and do things to him.

"Elliott," Michael said. "We're going to lose him. We have to get help. And, Elliott, we're going to lose you ..."

Elliott felt very hot—too hot. Michael took him under one arm, and carried E.T. under the other arm. He pulled them to the bathroom and put them in the shower. He had to put out this fire ...

The water came on and ran over Elliott and E.T. Michael went downstairs to Mary.

"Mom, I have to tell you something," he said.

He took her up to the bathroom, and Gertie followed. Mary looked in the shower, and closed her eyes. Then she opened them again. She saw Elliott and ...

"He's from the stars," said Gertie.

Mary pulled Elliott out of the shower.

"Downstairs, everybody," she said.

She pushed the children out of the bathroom. She couldn't think. The thing in the shower could stay there. She and the children had to get out.

Mary opened the front door. There was a scientist outside in white space-clothes. She closed the door quickly, and ran to a window. The scientist in white put **plastic** over the window so Mary couldn't open it. Then other scientists put plastic over the house, and it was closed.

plastic /ˈplæstɪk/ (n/adj) We make many things from *plastic*. We often carry food home from supermarkets in plastic bags.

CHAPTER 10

The Scientists

Elliott sat up in bed.
"E.T., don't go!" he cried.

B y nighttime the house was full of scientists and doctors. There were more scientists and police outside. Big lights shone down on the house. The only way in or out of the plastic was through a scientist's van.

The house was a hospital. Doctors looked at Mary and the children, and more doctors looked at E.T.

"The children taught the extra-terrestrial to talk," a doctor told Keys. "Seven or eight words."

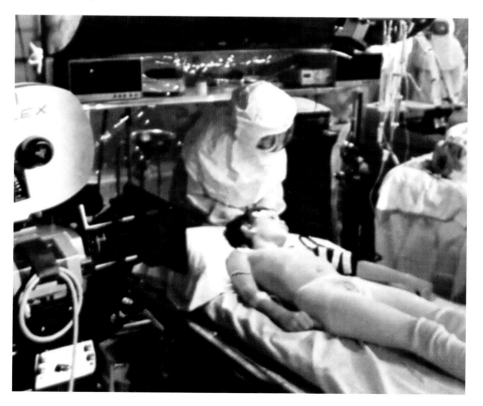

"*I* taught him," Gertie said.

"Does your friend feel anything?" Keys asked her. "Does he laugh or cry?"

"He cried," Gertie said. "He wanted to go home."

Keys opened a plastic door and went into another small room. He looked at E.T. and Elliott, and then at the doctors.

"Can you find his heart?" Keys asked the doctors.

"It's very difficult."

"Does he *have* a heart?" Keys asked.

"You see here? Maybe this is a heart, but it's too big ..."

The doctors did something to E.T., and Elliott, on the table next to him, could feel everything.

"You're hurting him. You're killing us ..." Elliott said.

Keys looked down at E.T.

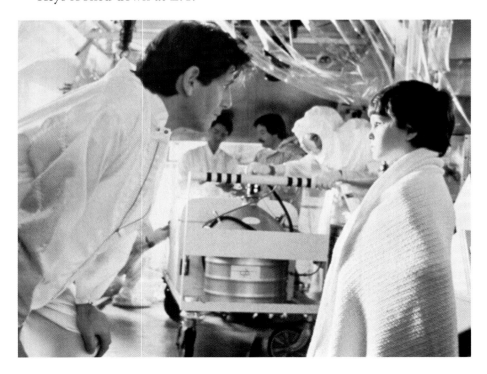

"Space people aren't beautiful," he thought. "They're very ugly. But this thing on the table is from the spaceship, and that's wonderful."

Keys wanted that spaceship.

"We're trying to help him, Elliott," he said. "He's sick."

"He wants to stay with me. He doesn't know you," Elliott told Keys.

"Elliott, your friend is very important to us, and we want to know him. He can teach us many things. You helped him and were good to him. We'll do that now, but you can stay with him."

Keys was wrong. Elliott couldn't stay with E.T. now. The old extra-terrestrial was near the end of his life. He could kill the Earth—and the people on it—and live. But no, he loved Earth, and he didn't want to do bad things. He wanted to go quietly.

"We're losing him ..." the doctors shouted. "Help!"

E.T.'s heart stopped. He was dead. At the same time, Elliott got strong again because E.T. wanted him to live.

Elliott sat up in bed.

"E.T., don't go!" he cried.

◆

Everybody left the room. The doctors put E.T. into a plastic bag, and then some scientists put him into a box.

Elliott looked down at E.T. and cried for him.

"I want you to stay with me. There are a million things here, and I want you to see them. Where are you now?"

geeple geeple snnnnnnnnnnnn org

Suddenly, a line of beautiful light shot through space. The light touched E.T.'s finger, and the finger started to shine. Then the old extra-terrestrial was full of the light, and his heart shone again.

Elliott saw the light and opened the plastic bag. He pulled the ice away from E.T.'s heart and saw it shine. He turned to the door and saw Keys with his mother. He quickly put his hand over the light.

E.T.'s eyes opened.

"E.T. phone home," he said.

"OK!" Elliott answered happily.

Elliott closed the bag again. Then he left the room and walked past Keys and his mother. He found Michael and told him about E.T. Michael made a phone call and quietly left the house.

◆

Elliott watched the scientists carry the box to the van outside the house. Then, they came back in.

"I'm going with E.T.," Elliott said.

Keys opened the door in the plastic wall and Elliott went through to the van. Michael was in the front of the van, and he was ready.

"Elliott," Michael said, "I only drove Mom's car near the house. I'm not very good …"

But he started the van. Suddenly, it shot down the road, through the policemen on their horses and the people around the house. The back of the van pulled the plastic from the front of the house.

Mary jumped into her car with Gertie and drove fast after the van. E.T. wasn't dead! The police drove after her—but she was very happy.

Activities 6

6.1 Were you right?

Look back at your answers to Activity 5.4. Then answer these questions.

Who:

1 gets sick, but doesn't die?

2 gets sick, dies, and comes back to life?

3 tells Elliott's mother about the spaceship?

4 shows E.T. to her?

5 drives E.T. away from the house?

6 follows the van, with Gertie?

6.2 What more did you learn?

Match the sentences to the people in the pictures.

1 He is afraid for Elliott.

2 He thinks that E.T. is ugly.

3 He tells Mary about E.T.

4 He wants to find the spaceship.

5 He wants to go with E.T.

6 He wants to know more about E.T.

7 He sees the light from space.

.3 Language in use

Look at the sentences on the right. Then finish the sentences below. Use the words at the end of the sentences.

> That night E.T. was **grayer**.
>
> Elliott felt **heavier** and **heavier**.

1 E.T. is .... than Elliott. (old)

2 Elliott is .... than E.T. (tall)

3 Elliott is feeling .... and .... than before. (hot, weak)

4 E.T.'s heart is .... now. (sad)

5 Keys thinks that E.T. is .... than Earth people. (ugly)

6 When E.T.'s heart stops, the room is suddenly .... (quiet)

7 After the light comes from space, E.T. feels .... (good)

8 When E.T. talks, Elliott feels .... (happy)

.4 What happens next?

Discuss these questions with other students. What do you think?

1 Who does Michael phone before he leaves the house (page 47)?
2 Why does he make the call?
3 What is his plan?
4 Will any of these help with his plan?

E.T. and the Spaceship

The spaceship was above them, with its warm lights. It was a million E.T.s—the most wonderful heart-light in the world.

The van stopped suddenly and Elliott and Michael helped E.T. out. Elliott's friends, Greg, Tyler, and Steve, looked at E.T. with big eyes.

"He's an extra-terrestrial," Elliott told them, "and we're taking him to his spaceship."

This was crazy. The boys couldn't understand anything, but they helped put E.T. onto Elliott's bike. Then, the boys rode away.

Tyler went first on his bike. His long legs went up and down. He looked back at E.T., and he rode very fast. What was that thing? He wanted to get away.

Later, the scientists found the van. Mary and the police were there, too. The scientists opened the van door, but there was nothing inside.

Suddenly, a little boy with red hair ran out of the trees near them.

"They took their bikes!" It was Lance. "The river—they're going to the river!"

The police and the scientists ran to their vans and cars and drove away.

Lance turned to Mary and said, "The forest—I'll show you."

"But—the river?"

"Listen," Lance said. "Maybe I'm strange, but I'm not stupid."

E.T. and the boys rode their bikes fast to the forest. E.T. could hear his friends in the spaceship.

"*znackle nerk nerk znackle*—do you hear us?"

"Yes, but please be quick—*zinggg zingle nerk nerk,*" E.T. answered.

The police and the scientists found nothing at the river. Then, on their radios, they heard the sounds of the extra-terrestrials. They followed those sounds.

"They're coming!" Michael shouted. He looked at Elliott.

The boys were on the last street before the forest. They rode as fast as they could. Then, they saw hundreds of police and scientists and their vans at the end of the street. The boys couldn't get past them to the forest.

"We'll go right into them," thought Elliott, "and that's the end."

But E.T. put up his finger and the bikes went up into the sky. Five bikes flew over the police and their cars and over the houses. E.T. looked down at the ground below. This was better. His heart-light shone again.

◆

Lance and Mary looked up at the bikes in the sky, and followed in Mary's car. Above the trees, Elliott flew quickly to the transmitter.

"There ..." E.T. pointed with his finger.

They came down to the ground and a beautiful light shone above Elliott. E.T. walked into the light with him and they looked up. The spaceship was above them, with its warm lights. It was a million E.T.s— the most wonderful heart-light in the world.

Elliott turned to E.T.

E.T. looked at the spaceship with big eyes. Then he looked at his friend, his helper.

"Thank you, Elliott ..." E.T. said. He was stronger now.

Mary came into the forest, and E.T. looked quietly at the beautiful woman. Gertie ran to him.

"Here are your flowers," she said.

E.T. took her in his arms.

"Be good," he said.

Then, they heard the sound of keys, and the scientist ran into the forest. E.T. quickly put Gertie down. He turned to Elliott and put out his hand.

"Come?" E.T. asked.

"Stay," Elliott said.

E.T. put his arms around the boy and felt sad. He touched Elliott on the head with his finger.

"I'll be right here," E.T. said, and his finger shone.

E.T. walked into the spaceship, and the light inside the ship shone above him. He felt the light inside him get brighter and brighter—and Elliott felt it, too. E.T.'s heart, and Elliott's, were not sad now—they were full of love.

E.T. went into the light, with his flowers.

Talk about it

1 **Work with another student. Have this conversation.**

Student A	You are Mary. You are standing next to Keys in the forest. The spaceship is flying away. Your children are feeling happy and sad at the same time. How are you feeling? What are you thinking about? Did your children do the right thing? Why? Tell Keys.
Student B	You are Keys. You are standing with Mary, and the spaceship is flying away. You really wanted to help E.T., too. You wanted to learn about his world and now you can't. How are you feeling? What are you thinking about? Tell Mary.

2 **Discuss these questions.**

a Are you happy with the end of the story? Why (not)?
b How will the children be different after the end of the story? Will their *lives* change, too?
c Will E.T. come back to Earth? Why (not)?

It is a year after the end of the story. E.T. visits Earth again. Elliott wants to give him things. E.T. can then take them to his world. They will help E.T.'s friends to understand more about Earth. What will tell them most about the lives of Earth people? Discuss these questions and then write down twenty things.

1. a computer game about life in space
2.
3.
4.
5.
6.
7.
8.
9.
10.
11.
12.
13.
14.
15.
16.
17.
18.
19.
20.

1 **Work with two or three other students.**

E.T. is a story about space, but it is also a story about friends.

  a Discuss other movies about good friends. Choose one movie and tell the story.

  b Do you have a very good friend? Talk about a difficult time in your life. What did your friend do for you? What *is* "a good friend"? Discuss your ideas.

2 **Learn about some famous American "Friends."**

  a Who are these people? What are their names in the television story? How did they meet? Do you know?

  b Look on the Internet. When did *Friends* start on American TV? When did it end? How many countries show it on TV now? Why do people like watching it?

  c Which "Friend" would you like to meet? Why?

3 **Help your neighbors.**

Work with the same other students. You all live on the same street. A family from out of town is moving in on the street. You would like to do something nice for the new people. You want to be good neighbors.

a What can you do? The pictures will give you some ideas, but think of more. Write them below.

....

....

....

....

....

....

....

....

....

....

b Discuss your ideas and then choose the best one.

c Make plans. How are you going to do this? What is the best time? What will each of you do? Make notes.

Notes

4 **Write to your new neighbors. Tell them about you and your family, and about your friends in the other houses. Tell them about life on the street. Then tell them about your plans. What do they think? Ask them.**

. . . .
. . . .
. . . .
. . . .
. . . .

Dear Mr. and Mrs. Smith,

[blank lined writing space]

With best wishes,

. . . .